HOW THE REINDEER SAVED SANTA

HOW THE REINDEER
SAVED SANTA

CAROLYN HAYWOOD

ILLUSTRATED BY
VICTOR AMBRUS

WILLIAM MORROW and COMPANY, INC. NEW YORK

Text copyright © 1986 by Carolyn Haywood

Illustrations copyright © 1986 by Victor Ambrus
All rights reserved.
No part of this book may be reproduced
or utilized in any form or by any means, electronic
or mechanical, including photocopying, recording or by any
information storage and retrieval system, without
permission in writing from the Publisher.
Inquiries should be addressed to
William Morrow and Company, Inc.,
105 Madison Avenue,
New York, NY 10016.
Printed in Hong Kong.
1 2 3 4 5 6 7 8 9 10

Library of Congress Cataloging-in-Publication Data
Haywood, Carolyn, 1898-
How the reindeer saved Santa.
Summary: Deciding that his sleigh is too old to use
for delivering presents, Santa Claus gets a helicopter
but finds after several mishaps that his sleigh and
reindeer are still the most reliable transportation.
[1. Santa Claus—Fiction. 2. Christmas—Fiction]
I. Ambrus, Victor G., ill.
III. Title.
PZ7.H31496Ho 1986 [E]   85-28456
ISBN 0-688-05903-1
ISBN 0-688-05904-X (lib. ed.)

Santa Claus had finished his toy making for this year, and Christmas would soon be here.

It was time for him to examine his sleigh. He didn't want it to break down on his Christmas Eve trip. Santa knew that his sleigh was getting old; after all, it was the only one he had ever had. He took out his magnifying glass to examine the sleigh more carefully. It was rusty in spots, and there were dents in the runners.

"My, oh, my," said Santa Claus, "I didn't realize the sleigh was in such bad shape. Perhaps I should get something more modern, one of those what-do-you-call-'ems that I see flying. A helicopter, I think it's called."

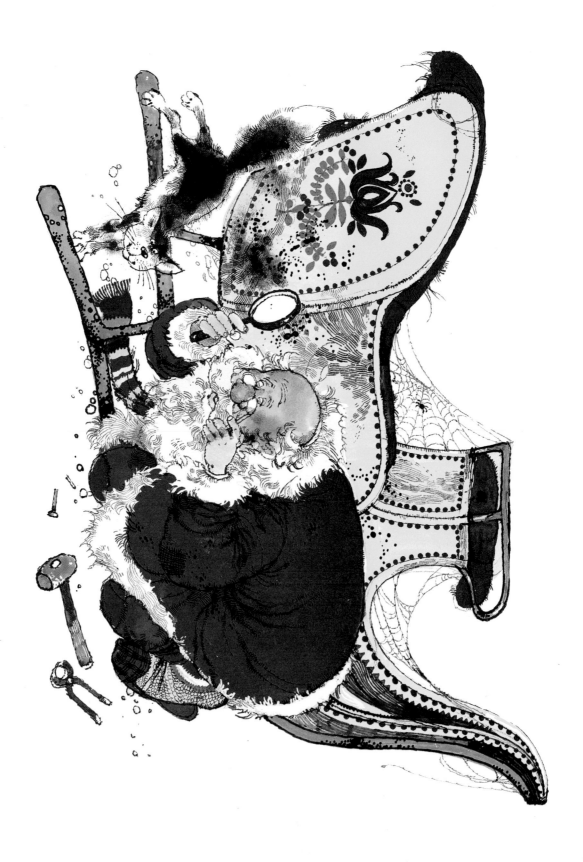

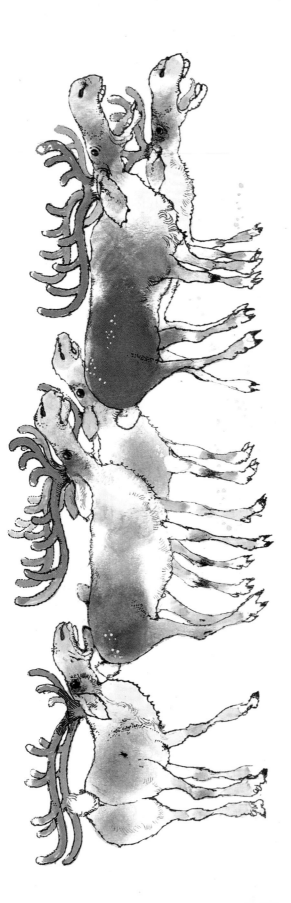

Then Santa Claus thought about his reindeer. The reindeer had been eating him out of house and home for years. They also had been doing a great deal of complaining:

"Santa Claus, it's too cold up here. Why can't we fly south for the winter?"

"Santa Claus, we don't like the mash you give us. Why can't we have the one that's advertised on TV?"

"Yes," Santa Claus decided. "The time has definitely come to put the reindeer out to pasture." He would miss them of course, but he was through with reindeer. He didn't want to be an old fogey. The sleigh and the reindeer would have to go.

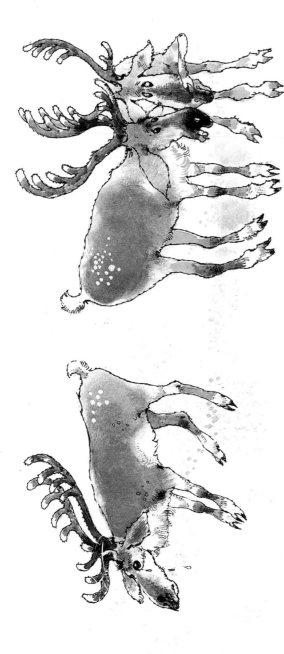

Santa Claus called the children's museum. He knew that children would have a wonderful time there crawling all over Santa's sleigh. He told the museum director that he was going to give the museum his sleigh and asked if they could send someone to pick it up right away. He wanted to be sure he wouldn't change his mind.

Santa Claus kept the sleigh bells. He couldn't bear to part with them. He would find a way to put them on his new helicopter.

He was sorry to say good-bye to his reindeer when he turned them out to pasture. Santa Claus cried and the reindeer cried. It was really a very wet day all around.

Santa Claus decided to order his helicopter over the telephone. When the phone was answered a voice said, "This is Mr. Helicopter. What can I do for you?"

"Oh, Mr. Helicopter, this is Santa Claus. I'd like to order a helicopter. I have given my sleigh to a museum."

"Santa Claus!" exclaimed Mr. Helicopter. "We have never had such an important customer. Our helicopter will be a gift to you, *our* Christmas gift. What color would you like?"

"White is *the* color up here at the North Pole," said Santa Claus. "But I would like Christmas decorations painted on the sides—my initials in the center of a green holly wreath with red berries. And if you add the words 'Merry Christmas' in red, I think it will be very attractive."

"Wonderful, wonderful," said Mr. Helicopter. "The most important paint job we've ever done."

"Mr. Helicopter," said Santa Claus, "thank you very much for this gift. When will it arrive?"

"Our special delivery boy will deliver it," said Mr. Helicopter. "He's my son. He was nine last Christmas," said Mr. Helicopter.

"You mean a boy who isn't even ten years old is flying my helicopter up to the North Pole?" said Santa Claus.

"Have no fear, Santa Claus," said Mr. Helicopter. "Joey will explain everything to you."

A few days later, the helicopter landed outside of Santa's toy shop. Joey Helicopter stepped out, and as he shook

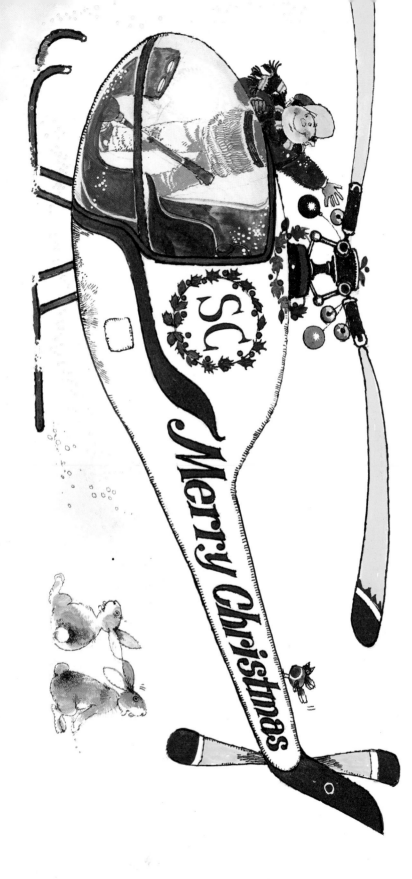

Santa's hand, he said, "This is a very important day for me. I'll go down in history as the boy who taught Santa Claus how to fly his helicopter."

Santa Claus gave the sleigh bells to Joey, and he fastened them to the door handle. "Now," said the boy, "let's go for a spin."

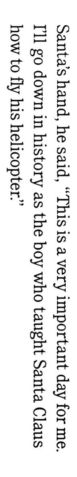

Santa Claus stepped into the helicopter and they took off. As they flew, Joey showed Santa Claus how to fly the machine. When they set down again at the North Pole the boy said, "Now *you* take it for a trial run."

As Santa Claus flew over a town two children looked up at the helicopter, and the little girl said, "I hear sleigh bells. It must be Santa Claus."

"It is not," said her brother. "Santa Claus comes at night, not during the day."

"I'm sure it's Santa," said the girl. "I can see the red tassel on his cap."

"I liked it better when he came in his sleigh with the reindeer," said her brother.

"Me, too," said his sister.

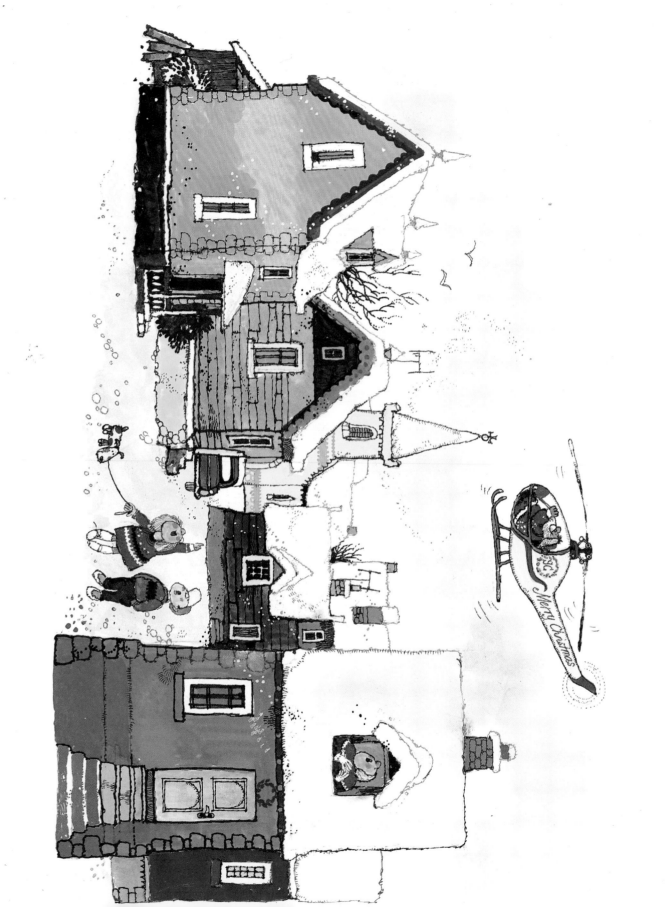

When Santa Claus returned to the North Pole, he said to Joey Helicopter, "I'll take you back to the factory now."

As Santa Claus let Joey out at the factory, the boy said, "Now, Santa Claus, don't lose the key to the door of the helicopter."

"Don't worry about me," Santa Claus replied. "I never lose anything. Do I ever lose any of the toys the children want?"

When Santa Claus reached home he decided to make a trial landing on the roof of his toy shop. "I must land this machine beside the chimney," he said to himself, "for it is down the chimney I go with the children's toys."

Santa Claus touched down on the roof, but the helicopter slid off into a large snowbank.

When Santa Claus saw his helicopter almost buried in the snow, he cried, "What am I to do? How will I get to the chimneys? I'll have to ring doorbells and say, 'Good evening, I'm Santa Claus. I've brought the toys for the children.'"

Santa Claus chuckled to himself. "I'll feel like a postman—not Santa Claus."

Santa Claus brought out his snow shovel and set to work digging his helicopter out of the snowbank. As he worked he began to think about his sleigh. Perhaps he had acted too hastily in giving it to the museum.

Then his thoughts turned to the reindeer and how every Christmas Eve they had carried him all over the world. The sleigh and the reindeer had always served him well.

When Santa Claus finished digging the helicopter out of the snowbank, he went into the toy shop to rest and have a cup of soup.

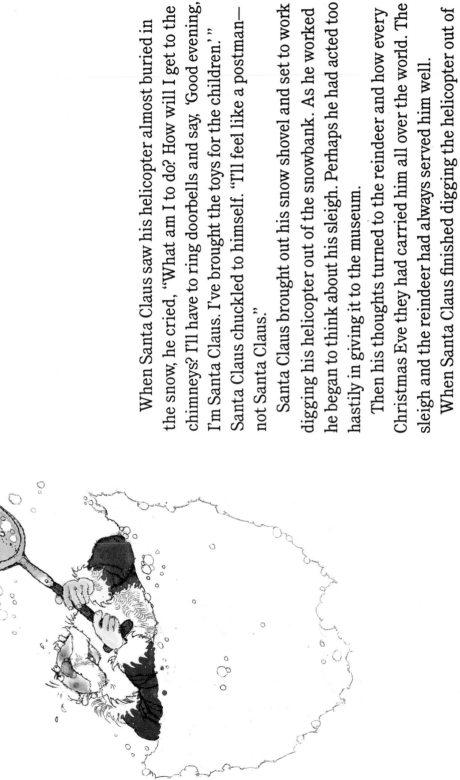

While he ate his soup he thought about how smoothly his sleigh had glided through the air. His sleigh and his reindeer never fell off the roof.

By the time Santa Claus had finished his soup he had decided to fly the helicopter down to the museum and ask for his sleigh back. He would give them the helicopter instead.

Santa Claus looked at his watch. "My goodness," he cried, "it's Christmas Eve. The children are already asleep in their beds, and here am I still at the North Pole."

Santa Claus picked up his bag of toys and hurried to his helicopter. As he took the key out of his pocket to open the door, it slipped out of his hand and fell into the snow. Santa Claus knew at once that he would never find it. He jumped up and down, exclaiming, "Oh, what shall I do? What shall I do?" Now Santa Claus was in real trouble, and no one was around to help him. No one.

But the reindeer in the pasture heard his cries, and they came running. "What's the matter, Santa Claus?" they said. "I'm in trouble," he exclaimed. "I want to fly this helicopter down to the museum and get my sleigh back, but I've dropped the key into the snow."

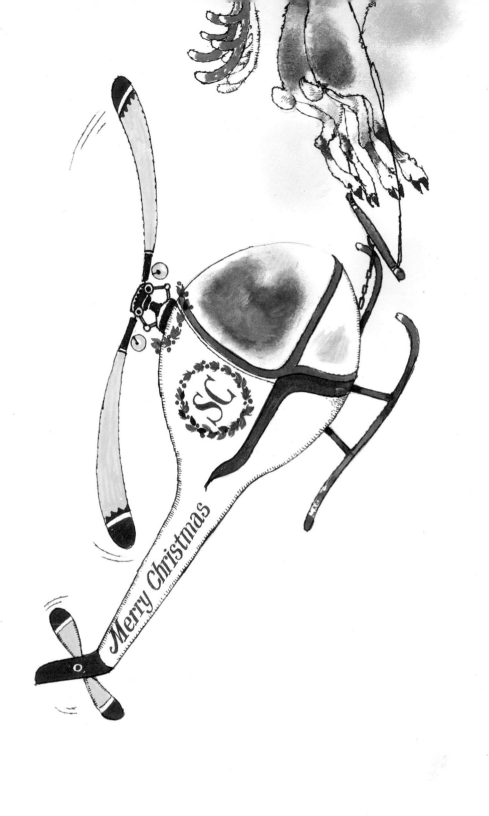

Prancer said, "Don't worry Santa Claus, we'll help you. Just fasten our harness to the helicopter, and away we'll go."

"But I have to go, too," said Santa Claus.

"You can ride on my back," Prancer said. "Off we go."

The sleigh bells jingled as they flew.

When they arrived at the museum Santa Claus explained his problem, and they agreed to take the helicopter in exchange for Santa's sleigh.

THE ORIGINAL
SLEIGH
Used by Santa Claus
Every Christmas
until recently.
Please touch if you
want to!

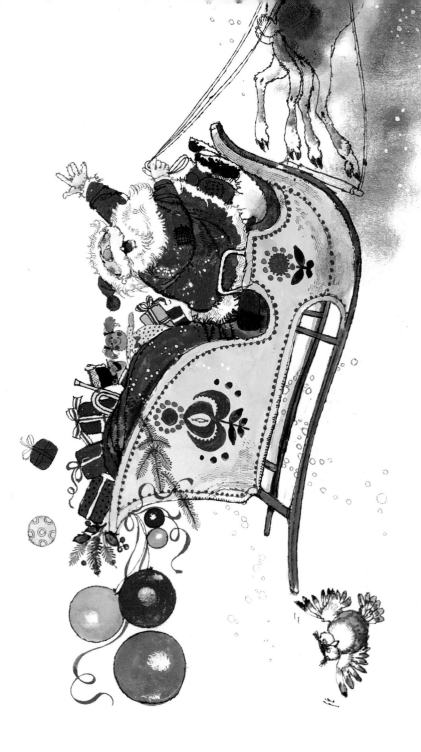

Santa Claus patted each reindeer as he hitched them up to the sleigh.

Nothing could ever take the place of his sleigh and reindeer.

Just as the clocks struck midnight the reindeer flew off with Santa Claus and his pack of toys.

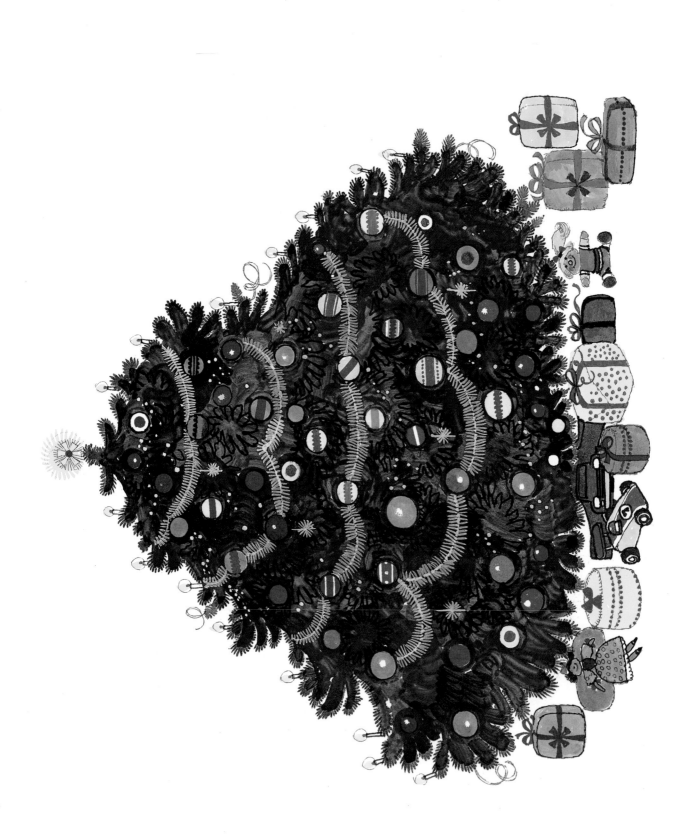

Now that Santa Claus could make his trip, toys were under every Christmas tree and a jolly Christmas was enjoyed by children everywhere!